Roohi and Khidr

Orange Books Publication

1st Floor, Rajhans Arcade, Mall Road, Kohka, Bhilai, Chhattisgarh 490020

Website: **www.orangebooks.in**

First Edition, 2025

ISBN: 978-93-6554-811-2

Price: Rs. 220.00

Printed in India

ROOHI & KHIDR

A Search for Love, Guided by the Wisdom of Rumi

PARUL SHARMA

Orange Books Publication
www.orangebooks.in

This book is dedicated to

My parents and teachers for giving me

The wings to reach out for my dreams,

My daughter for inspiring me to dream bigger,

Grandparents for instilling in me a love for the arts,

And all my family members, friends and well-wishers

for their unwavering support.

I remain ever grateful and indebted to them.

Preface

Dear Reader,

Firstly, I thank you for holding this book in your hands. This book is my labour of love and trust; love for the art of writing and trust that this book will connect us. No matter to what degree and extent, it is this connection between you and me, the writer and the reader, which holds a sacred place in my heart, and I trust that this book builds the same between us.

It will be of interest to you to know that writing this book was a serendipitous experience for me. I did not really set out to write this book. In fact the book began with some prose pieces that I wrote to articulate an inspiration. I have always been deeply inspired by Rumi's poetry. As I finished writing those prose pieces, I observed a unique connection between them and a few of Rumi's quotes/poems that I had previously read. This observation in turn led me to build up a story, and that is how I ended up writing this book. Through this story, I have endeavoured to express my understanding and perspective on some of Rumi's thoughts, which the story will reveal. This book is, therefore, as much a gift to me as it is to you, and I feel honoured to bring it to you.

This is the story of Roohi and Khidr, about their quest for the deeper meaning of life and the soul-awakening and life-transforming adventure that unfolds when they meet each other. Their falling in love is only the beginning of that adventure.

I hope you enjoy being a part of this quest.

With Love,

Parul

"The soul is a stranger trying to find a home,
somewhere that is not a where."

-Rumi, The Big Read Book

Contents

A Windy Sunset

I was sitting at the window of my house, watching from my table, the tangerine sun about to set soon beyond the mountains. I moved aside my notebook to witness the miracle of nature about to unfold in the sky. The azure sky began to acquire varied hues. Turquoise, golden, pink, amber, I gaped at the resplendent fluid colours floating in the sky.

It was windier than usual. The air had acquired a tinge of coldness, a hint of the fast - approaching winters.

It had been seven months since I had left my home in an urban city to realise my dream of writing a book amidst nature.

I lived alone in the vicinity of jungles, homesteading in a remote mountainous region, with minimal things necessary for human survival. My fortnightly visit to a distant town for groceries and essentials was the only social contact I had in my life, apart from occasional visits I would make to a kind farmer's family living a few miles away. I felt quite at peace with my reclusive, quiet life in the middle of the mountains.

Simfi

As I looked outside the window, Simfi constantly trotted around my feet and her fluffy fur brushed against my toes. Simfi was a large female mountain dog who became my companion since my first visit to this house.

When I was walking the trail to my house for the very first time to move there, I noticed a feeble but constant sound of footsteps following me. I was walking alone on a deserted trail, so the sound was unexpected.

When I looked back and tried to trace the sound attentively, I discovered a large, furry, creamy white colored mountain dog (whom I would later name Simfi) following me from a distance. When her eyes met my inquisitive gaze, we both gave each other a trusting look.

I marvelled at the charming beauty of the dog in my mind and carried on with my walk, thinking that the dog would eventually leave somewhere on the way. But contrary to what I had expected, Simfi never left my side and accompanied me till we reached the house. When I looked back at her on reaching, she was standing behind me, moaning softly and wagging her tail.

When Simfi refused to leave, I squatted down to look into her big, wondrous eyes. Her eyes, pristine and innocent, seemed to sing a harmonious 'symphony' of joy and friendship to me. I thus named her 'Simfi' and hugged her warmly. We have lived together in the house since then.

She was not a pet to me but a friend, a confidant and a companion who brought laughter to my otherwise monotonous quiet routine.

Simfi, like a true mountaineer, was free-spirited and never stayed in the house continuously. She liked to walk around with me, but would at times wander alone in the jungles and mountains during the day and usually return in the evening. At times, her solo outings would last for a few days, but she eventually always returned. I believed her to be a divine gift to me.

My Bond with Maulana

Gazing at the sky, I drifted into the memories of the days that led me to my present life. The day I was leaving my erstwhile home, I carried with me only a few essential possessions, which were absolutely necessary for my life and gave me a sense of purpose.

Rumi's teachings were one of, if not the most important, amongst them. Whenever I had felt confused or distraught with situations in life, it had always been Rumi whom I had turned to. I liked to refer to him as 'Maulana' (as he is widely called), which means 'the Master' because he was truly my master or guide in life. Reading his words brought me ease, a sense of tranquil and faith that everything was impermanent in this world and that things, no matter how difficult, always turned out alright at the end.

Rumi had left the physical world in the 13th century, but for me, he was still very much alive. Traversing centuries, I believed the lanes of Konya, Turkey, still echoed with Maulana's divine poems. I imagined Konya with Rumi's verses reverberating across oceans and continents, his *Sama*[1] gatherings still resounding sonorously and his dervish pupils whirling in the eternal dance of sublime ecstasy. To me, it felt as if those divine verses were whispered into the winds flowing from Konya and that one just had to 'tune in' to them to immerse in their soul-stirring wisdom.

Maulana was so alive in my heart that his quotes and poems consistently flashed in my mind whenever I needed any guidance or direction in my life. His teachings were as if a part of my heart and psyche.

In my humble travel bag, thus, I carried with me teachings of Rumi- collated in my numerous notes, writings, quotes, booklets, books, thesis and so on.

Although I had set out on my journey to write my book, I had no idea what it was really going to be about. But something in my heart said that it would be inspired in some inexplicable way by the wisdom of Rumi.
"Your heart knows the way. Run in that direction"

I would often remember this quote by Rumi, and would thus continue to 'remember' and walk towards the 'calling of my heart'.

---

[1] Spiritual whirling dance of Sufis

Doubt

Delving further in the memory of those days, I remembered how hesitant my mother was to let me go. She was concerned about my safety, just like any mother would be in her situation.

When I was about to leave, she asked me worriedly, “Do you know what you're going to write about? Do you know what people want to read? Do you even know what a writer’s life is all about?”

I knew my mother loved me and had no intention to instil doubts in my heart, yet love, when intertwined with attachment, makes us hurt the very person we deeply love.

I replied calmly, “I don’t know what a writer’s life is all about, and I want to discover it for my own self. Although I do not know what I am going to write and for whom I am going to write it, I know I will write it for my own self more than for anyone else. And in finding my own voice, I hope others will find theirs too.”

Overcome with emotions, my mother asked me with welled-up eyes, “You are just a 21-year-old! How will you do life all alone?”

I replied, hugging my mother, “Don’t worry, mum! You have raised me well to trust my heart and live by it.”

And thus, with Maulana’s words as my guide, I began my solitary journey as a writer on a quest to discover myself.

A Knock

Lost thus in the memories of past, a sudden gale of winds returned me to the present moment. My gaze fell from the neon orange sky on to my cream coloured notepad on the table. Incoherent handwritten notes, pencil scribbling, side notes, clipped references, hurried rough drafts; my scattered writings on the notepad were as sporadic as my thoughts waiting to be streamlined.

Just next to the notepad was kept a red coloured velvet untitled book which contained commentary on numerous quotes of Maulana. Much like a precious gemstone kept away from the public glare, I had purchased this book from an old, quaint bookstore located at a hidden corner of the city.

A strong gale of cold wind gushed through the window, flipping the pages of the book. When the gale stopped, the book remained open to a page. I went closer and the page read:

"Often do we waste time seeking answers to questions,
while the answers lie within the questions themselves;

Just like someone who keeps knocking at the door,
without realising that he is already within the house."

Just as I read these lines, I heard a knock at the door. Dumbfounded, I gasped at the unexpected coincidence.

It had been a long time since anyone had knocked at my door. "Who could it be? Did I just imagine the knock?" I wondered when I heard a gentle knock once again.

Question and Answer

My heart pounded with the feelings of fear, confusion, doubt and hesitation. With shaky feet I moved near the door and almost whispered, "Who is it?"

"It is I", replied a gentle husky male voice.

Taken aback by the unusual reply, I repeated, louder this time, "Who is it?"

My fear probably was too evident in my tone as the reply came in an even softer, almost pleading tone, "I am sorry to bother you, Miss! I am a wanderer who has got lost in these jungles. It was after a long, arduous trail that I was able to spot a sign of habitation, and that was your house. I require some water and shelter for some time, if possible. I promise you, I will not cause any inconvenience to you. I seek mercy from you, Miss, from a human to a human." I could hear him breaking into tears as he ended his sentence.

His painful, honest voice pierced my heart. I could wait no more and instantly opened the door.

The Introduction

As I opened the door, stood before me a tall, strongly built young man, dressed in a coarse off-white robe fastened at the waist. He had sharp, chiselled features and long black hair that touched his shoulders. Thick eyebrows, rugged facial hair and broad forehead, he stood before me with his eyes lowered. Bending towards me, probably due to fatigue, his face looked tired and dusty. His robe was even worn off in some places. But even in this distraught state, he looked divinely handsome.

“Thank you”, he muttered, bending further.

I looked back, Simfi was standing steadfast, looking into my eyes with confidence, as if reassuring me that there was nothing to be worried about.

“Sit please”, I said to the man, pointing at the wooden armchair opposite the window.

The sun had not set yet, and as the man sat on the chair, faint orange sunrays passing through the window panes fell on his face, illuminating his pale brown complexion. His visage glowed like that of a man with deep wisdom.

He was probably as old as or only a little older than me, but the deep lines on his forehead made him look older. Small bruises and cuts on his face, seemingly from his long and difficult travel, shone in the sunlight. Dirt and sweat were stuck stubbornly on his skin. But beyond this rugged demeanour, his majestic and calm persona was hard for me to ignore.

Offering him a tumbler of water, I sat on a humble jute stool at a short distance from him.

He quickly gulped down the water and licked his chapped lips. A sense of relief visibly took over him, and for the first time, he raised his eyes.

He looked towards me, probably to thank me, but his deep gaze instantly locked my eyes. Our eyes remained transfixed at each other for a few moments, which seemed longer than aeons. His gaze had an unfathomable depth, and I felt absolutely exposed and vulnerable in front of him. He suddenly withdrew his gaze, evidently conscious, swallowing down his throat the words he had presumably wished to utter.

We sat down still in silence, our eyes lowered, quietly accepting how deeply we felt drawn to each other. I suddenly cleared my throat and asked, “What is your name?”

Seemingly grateful to me for having broken the ice, he answered softly, “My name is Khidr. And if I may ask, what is yours?”

His voice no longer had the shiver of hesitation but a reassurance of friendship. He spoke as if he weren’t a stranger but a friend to me.

“Khidr: ‘the guide of souls’” I muttered the meaning of his name in my mind.

I smiled at him and replied, “That’s such a lovely name. My name is Roohi. It means ‘soul’.”

He nodded in agreement. We smiled at each other with childlike innocence. I was surprised how familiar Khidr felt to me, although he was a complete stranger. The sun set outside the window, leaving a blush of coy redness on our cheeks.

“What has brought you here, Khidr? What is your introduction?” I asked.

“My introduction?” he sounded unsure.

“U-hmm”, I prompted him to answer.

“If I answer your question, Roohi, I will have to remember all that I have set out to forget: my name, my possessions, my qualifications, my identities, which others had given me or which I had acquired on others’ insistence. And I do not wish to remember them again. I have left everything behind to discover who I really am, beyond these acquired identities. I am as unaware of my introduction as you are. I can only say that I am a seeker in search of my true self. Is this enough?"

I nodded slowly. Simfi watched over our conversation attentively with her ears raised, as if she understood every word of it.

After a pause, Khidr continued, "If this introduction doesn't make you comfortable with my presence, I will be glad to take your leave, Roohi. You have been very kind to me, and I do not in any way wish to cause you any inconvenience."

"Quite the contrary, Khidr", I answered, "Your introduction in reality, introduces me too. I feel I am no more alone in my journey of self-discovery; there is someone else too who is walking a path similar to mine. I am happy I could meet you"

It was getting dark, and I had to prepare a meal.

"You must be very tired. There is water kept over the fire pit outside, which I lit a while ago. You may freshen yourself there. I will get the food ready," I stood up, handing him a spare towel and moving outside to prepare the meal. Simfi followed me towards the stove.

The Supper

I was not a deft cook but was reasonably good at cooking. There was a makeshift kitchen with coal stove just outside the house and I prepared a quick meal of soup, porridge and lentils. The appetizing aroma of spices, burning coal and cereals flowed all around the house. Simfi was wagging her tail swiftly, apparently happy with my preparation.

I served her meals at a corner and quickly moved to take the cooked hot meals inside the house. As I turned, Khidr was standing in front of me.

He had washed his dusty robe, which was hanging for drying at the back. Wearing a pair of loose pants, he had covered his broad torso with the towel draped like a shawl.

Bathed clean, washed off the dirt and sweat, his wet, long hair neatly spread over his shoulder, he shone like the moon in the darkness of night. I smiled at him as he offered to help me take the food inside the house. Simfi, having finished her food, watched us smugly.

Having arranged the food and read our prayers, we ate to our hearts' content. I was so happy to share my meals with someone after a long time. Khidr had a charming grace in the way he had food, savouring each morsel with attentiveness and absorbing its taste deeply. How satiated I felt at seeing him eat delightfully! The contented innocent smile on his face was the highest compliment I had ever received for my cookery.

We both ate together almost silently, exchanging a few merry words, timid chuckles of laughter here and there and sharing an unspoken camaraderie of tranquil and peace.

It was a cold and breezy night outside, yet we felt cosy and safe in this little house, eating our warm supper together.

Gratitude

As we finished eating our meals, Khidr began to thank me once again but I interrupted him midway.

"Thank me no more, Khidr, for I am as grateful to you as you are to me. Your company has made my heart full today. In offering you shelter, my house looks like a home, in feeding you supper, my belly feels satiated, and in offering you warmth, my stove glows brighter. In sharing your story, you have given a meaning to mine, in speaking your truth, you have revealed mine, and in exposing your pains, you have healed mine. How shall I be able to thank you enough?" A drop of tear slipped from the corner of my eye.

As I lifted my head, I saw Khidr wiping his eyes too. We nodded at each other with a humble smile and moved outside to wash our utensils. I looked around for Simfi, but she was nowhere to be seen.

Moon and the Flame

As we stepped out to wash the utensils, I realized it had turned colder and windier outside. I moved towards the fire pit to adjust the logs and increase the flame. The flame glistened and leapt high, soaring towards the full moon, which had risen to its full glory in the dark sky. The darkness of night was swept over by the silver shine of moonlight and the golden glow of flames. Dark shadows of cypress trees, wheezing winds, crackle of fire flames and the moon watching over from above; the night had a mystical charm about itself.

The trees were constantly whistling in the strong thrust of winds. A gust of cold gale blew, and I saw Khidr mildly shivering with cold. I quickly walked closer to him. Stretching my toes to reach his height, I tried to spread my shawl over his shoulders. A sudden shove of the strong winds pushed me ahead, and the next moment I found myself in his warm embrace.

His face shone softly in the light of the fire. The colour of his eyes, hazel brown, which I saw for the first time from such closeness, appeared like caramel melted in the warmth of the fire. I saw my reflection in his eyes. My hair had escaped from the grip of the bun and had intermingled with his flowing tresses. I watched each feature of his face intently as he embraced me closer with affection. My shawl had wrapped both of us. And just like the raindrops that flow seamlessly on a flower's petals, our lips slipped onto each other's.

Our eyes closed, we held on to each other under the full moonlight, listening to the rhythmic crackling of flames, and time seemed to stand still.

Silhouette of Silence

Night set in and it turned chilly. We were still standing in the lap of nature, enveloped in my shawl. The ever-vigilant mountains had shut their eyes, as if persuading us to move inside.

As we returned to the house, the cold window panes crackled with the force of the winds and the curtains swung wildly. Surrounding woods enveloped in the density of darkness, a silhouette of silence formed inside the room, making every sound strangely distant; the sound of birds, the sound of winds, the sound of trees, the sound of our breaths.

Desire paced our breaths and tightened our embrace. Next moment we were lying close to each other. The silhouette of silence engulfed us as we breathed under the blanket. It was dark, so dark that we could no longer see each other, and yet strangely, we could, in a sense, much deeper than we had ever before. Our sense of touch as if evolved into a surreal vision. We ran our fingers exploring each other's naked forms. But we no longer felt but rather saw each other through our touch, in depths that no light could ever reveal.

Sucked into a vacuum of nothingness, we watched the lines dividing our bodies blur into the silhouette of silence, as we discovered the common epicentre of our shared existence.

The Dawn

When I woke up the next day, I knew I woke up with a smile. I stretched my hands to touch Khidr but he was not there.

As I sat up, I found Simfi looking at me across the bed. Her furry ears were stiff and upright, her tail lethargic, and her eyes seemed lost. This was not how she looked in the mornings. I immediately sensed that something was not right.

I went around the house looking for Khidr, but he was nowhere to be seen. I ran outside to search for him. There was a deafening silence in the air. The sun had risen, the winds did not blow anymore, and the fire pit had died down. His robe was not hanging where it was last night and my shawl that he had worn last night was lying near the fire pit, neatly folded. He had clearly left.

My heart sank, and I felt a plume of grief rising in my chest. I collapsed on the ground. Simfi fervently tried to comfort me, wagging her tail vigorously and licking my hands.

Screeching a howl of pain, I shrieked aloud his name that echoed in the mountains. The landscape reverberated with the name of Khidr. The silent cypress trees seemed to grieve along with me.

Grief

I spent the next several days hunting high and low for my beloved. I lost the sense of time, place and hunger. Dishevelled and distraught, I wandered in the surrounding mountains calling out his name aimlessly. I felt I had introduced his name to all the nearby jungles, mountains, trails and streams and that they too echoed my calls to Khidr.

Every morning, I would leave the house with renewed hope to search for Khidr, wandering and tracing every nook, trail and pathway. I would call out his name towards the sky, amidst trees, along the streams, looking at birds, sitting with flowers, in fervent faith that someone would convey my message, my longing, my ache to Khidr.

I wandered along in the desolate jungles, accompanied by Simfi who followed me at every step like a loyal friend. Whenever I felt tired, I would look back at her to seek assurance, but something in her eyes told me that I should return home. Probably, she knew that Khidr would not be found, at least for the time being. And in hindsight, I think I knew it too, but just didn't want to accept it. "You have to keep breaking your heart until it opens", in due course, Maulana's words guided me again. I realised I could not run away from the discomfort of longing, for it was the only cure for my pain. Taking his cue, I decided to wait for Khidr.

Wait

And so I waited. Days turned to weeks and weeks to months until I lost the count. I resignedly shut myself off from the world. Closing my heart, I locked in its deep chambers Khidr's presence, making it a part of my blood, flesh and bones. His presence lingered inside me, like the fragrance of an incense stick that could be felt in a closed room long after it had burned out.

He became a part of me, and the entire existence around me became a part of him. The soft sunlight touched me like his gentle kiss, leaves rustled like his whispers in my ears and winds blew like his fingers were playing with my hair.

When the pain of missing Khidr became too hard to bear, it started seeping on the pages through my ink. My thoughts, which were disarrayed so far, suddenly found their rhythm. As I started writing, all I could see was the ruminant hue of longing embossed in varied shapes, lines, contours and forms on my writing pad.

Writing about Khidr only made me realise how much I missed him.

A Search

My wait continued for a very long time until the day I could wait no longer.

The clouds floating on the mountains suddenly grew thicker that day and it started pouring. Dusk was yet to fall, yet it felt as if darkness was descending from the sky along with rain, seeping into every pore of existence, an unquenchable thirst. The landscape drenched in darkness howled with the thirst of longing.

The rains evoked a call in my heart, echoed by the mountains, rivers, winds and trees around. An echo so loud, it thud inside the core of my being. I suddenly stood up following the sound of the echo, for I knew it would lead me to Khidr. And thus began my search to find him once again.

A Journey

I knew in my heart, Khidr was waiting for me as earnestly as I was for him and that I had to take action and not merely wait.

In the wee hours of the next day, with some basic supplies packed in my small bag, I set out on the journey to find Khidr. I looked around for Simfi, but she was nowhere to be seen. Accepting it as the will of God, I decided to embark on the journey all alone.

“What you seek is seeking you”, Maulana had said, and as I began my search, I felt as if I was not alone after all. The gush of water streams, the map of constellations, contours of mountains, the direction of winds, the entire cosmos was as if leading me to him, leading me to my home.

The Fear

It had been hours since I had begun my search. The green trails and sporadic vegetation soon grew denser and darker. The trees became loftier and wider. I continued to wade my way through the lush, dark jungle. Although the thick shade of dense trees and the dark clouds in the sky made it tough to differentiate the day from the night, I could sense that it was still daytime. I suddenly stumbled over a boulder hidden beneath the dense foliage. Caught unawares, I lost my balance and fell down, hitting my forehead with a sharp edge of the rock.

As I touched my wound, a greasy blob of blood wet my fingers. A sharp surge of pain reverberated through my body, and I released a helpless squeal of pain. The darkness grew darker, and I feebly collapsed on earth.

Helpless, I felt a tide of fear surging in my body. The mountains, the trees, the shrubs, all of which had seemed like friends to me some time ago, suddenly appeared like distant onlookers. I felt utterly desolate and desperate in my journey. A stream of tepid tears rolled down my cheeks.

As I blankly stared at the dark shade of thick, lofty trees, a ray of bright sunlight suddenly slanted through their leaves. Dense grey clouds made way for the azure sky, and the landscape was filled with the pink shades of approaching evening.

Bathed in the sunshine of the golden hour, the trees and shrubs acquired a yellow tinge. That warmth of sunlight felt like a balm on my wound. A faint smile resurfaced on my chapped lips. I was filled with hope again.

"The wound is the place where the light enters you", I smiled, remembering Maulana's words.

A Ray of Hope

I woke up the next day with the morning sunshine falling on my face. As I opened my eyes, the jungle was bathed in morning misty fog, mixing with the bright rays of the rising sun. My wound on the forehead had miraculously healed except for a scanty bruise remaining.

I rose to continue my journey ahead. No matter how hard the steps, no matter how tenuous the trail, the hope to meet Khidr kept propelling me ahead. His words, his smile, his embrace, his memories, pushed me beyond the most arduous obstacles. I had no plan, no roadmap laid out in front of me, but I continued walking quietly with an inexplicable faith in my heart, a faith so strong that no doubt could ever overshadow it.

Slowly but steadily, I would walk without taking any pause, drinking water from the streams and rivers, eating whatever I could manage to sustain my survival and lying down on rugged foliage when exhausted.

I continued walking like this on and on for days together. My body was getting frailer by the day. The little supplies I had carried were depleting. But a strange force stopped me from turning backwards. My feet knew only one direction, onward and forward.

Serendipity

Countless days had passed since I had embarked on this journey. Memories of my house, my garden, my erstwhile life, all seemed hazy in my mind, but memories of Khidr refused to fade. It was perhaps the only thing that remained clear in my comprehension; everything else had become like a foggy film reeling on the screen of my mind from time to time. Depleting energy levels, blistered feet, frail body had gravely affected my cognitive abilities. My chances of surviving this journey began to look bleak.

Suddenly, it started to pour heavily, a thunderstorm followed, and the sky roared with lightning. My already frail body began to tremble uncontrollably. When I opened my eyes, I realised I had lost consciousness. Dishevelled, I looked around trying to regain my sense of balance. Suddenly out of nowhere, I spotted a faint track across a little distance, leading to somewhere. “A track in the middle of this desolate, dense jungle!” A wave of curiosity swept over me. I was filled with hope that all was not lost yet. Perhaps I will find some shelter and warmth to keep me alive until I find my destiny.

The curiosity instilled a revived vigour into my otherwise dampened spirits.

“As you start to walk on the way, the way appears.” Maulana’s words flashed in my mind, and I nimbly began to walk towards the track.

The Path

The track felt farther than what it had appeared to me. I started walking faster and eventually began to run towards it. No matter how fast I ran, it seemed to go farther away and always stayed beyond my reach. Panting, I paused to catch a breath. As I stopped, I was surprised to see that the track had disappeared. Flabbergasted, I looked around as if something somewhere would give me a clue about this mystery. But of course, there was nothing and no one to help me except the quiet nature staring at me in blank anticipation. Unsure and confused, I took a step in the same direction where I had last seen the track. As I took the step, miraculously enough, the track reappeared, in the same direction where it was before I had paused.

Although the track was still distant, I was overjoyed to see it reappear. I began to move slowly and cautiously towards it. Each slow step I took towards it made the track look even clearer and closer. I slowly treaded towards it, and it started looking even more coherent and clearer. Excited to see the path clearly unfolding, I decided to quicken my pace. But much to my surprise, as soon as I hurried, the path disappeared again.

I now understood well, and paced my walk with patience and calm. As I walked slowly with trust, the path continued to become more coherent and clearer. I slowly reached the path and started walking on the track.

I was now confident that with steady and patient steps, I would not lose the path again, for the path needs the traveller, as much as the traveller needs the path.

A Wall

I kept walking on the path in the hope to find some sign of habitation. I needed shelter of a home, even if for a short while, I needed someone to talk to, even if only niceties, I needed cooked food, even if a morsel.

As I walked, I suddenly saw a heavy mist descending onto the path ahead. On walking further, the mist thickened and visibility deteriorated. At a distance I saw something that appeared like a wall. Hoping it to be the end of the path, and probably a boundary leading to a house, I stretched my hand to touch the wall, when I heard a voice behind me.

“What are you looking for, dear Child? Come, this is the way,said the voice.

Startled, I looked back.

Looking Behind

Behind was standing an old saintly figure, smiling faintly. Pale complexioned, grey air, mediocre height, frail frame, his long silver beard flowed until his chest. He was dressed in a loose ivory white robe and wore a vertical long cap.

And his eyes? I had never seen such magnetic eyes before in my life. Deep as an ocean, illuminated as stars and mysterious as mountains, I felt so insignificant looking into his magnanimous eyes.

"If my revered Maulana were alive today, he would have looked the same." I thought awe-inspired. "But he left his physical body centuries ago. Who is this wise gentleman?"

Before I could say anything, the saint, stretching his hands benevolently, invited me towards his direction and said,

“Come this way, dear Child! Do not bother. I do not care about your introduction, your past or present. I do not care about your mistakes or accomplishments. You are enough here. Take shelter under the arms of this tree. Rest for a while. There are no judgments, there are no questions, but there is only love in the kingdom of God.”

The saint’s peaceful words instantly calmed me. Much to my surprise, not only did the saint look like Maulana but also spoke like him in his own calm and reassuring voice. His voice, sweet, kind and gentle, evoked such deep emotions of surrender in me that I instantly knelt before him and started crying.

The saint came closer to me and touched my head to comfort me. Tired, confused and overwhelmed, I looked at him, pointing in the opposite direction and asked, “I saw a wall here. Is there a door to the beyond? Do you have your home here?”

I instantly winced at how silly my question sounded, but Baba answered with the same patience.

“There is no wall and there is no door. It is the mist which creates the illusion. And can there be a home better than the shelter of this tree?” The saint asked, looking up at the vast expanse of the overlooking cedar tree.

I looked up hesitantly and whispered, “Pardon me, I am so distressed. I must tell you a little about myself”

“Bother not, Child, I know everything and yet I need not know anything”, the saint smiled mystically.

Return

"You are saying 'this is the way'...You are asking me to return towards my home? But I have come such a long way," I asked the saint, perplexed.

"Oh, Child! We often have to wander somewhere very far to reach somewhere very close," the saint replied with poise.

I looked at the saint with earnest eyes. He gave me hope like a lighthouse would give to a drowning swimmer, in the middle of dark seas. I felt I had finally found a guide, a master, a guru to help me navigate through the quagmire of thoughts that swarmed my mind.

The Discourse

Before I could think of a suitable name to address him, his deferential persona made me impulsively call him '*Baba*'[2].

"Baba! I have been searching for my beloved for countless days. My heart burns in the agony of this separation. While the ache of any other wound eases with time, this ache of separation only increases with each passing day", I paused teary-eyed.

Baba nodded at me sympathetically and said, "Dear Child! If it were in my power, I would do anything to ease your pain, but as you rightly said, this is no ordinary pain. This pain has to be endured, for the cure

[2] 'Baba' is a term of respect, used in many cultures of South Asia to address elderly men

of this pain is in the pain itself. No other sickness compares to the sickness of the heart. It is only this way of pain which leads one to love.

But, please do not lose your heart, Child! Remember, it is this very pain which will liberate you from all the barriers that lie between you and the love you seek."

"Where there is ruin, there is hope for treasure" Baba's words reminded me of Maulana's verse.

"But why must I suffer this pain? Why love comes only to those who endure?" I asked.

"My Child! It is *love* you seek and not some ordinary pleasure, it is truth you seek and not a false pretence, it is the real you seek and not a mirage. You crave the authentic in this illusory *dunya*[3]. You thirst for divine waters in the desert of materialism. And you expect it to come to you without endurance? Now tell me, how could this journey not be difficult? Remember, dear Child, that on the path of love, every hurt is a blessing."

Baba's words felt like a salve on my wounded heart. They were helping me find some clarity amidst the fog of doubts and worries I had caught myself in. Pondering over Baba's words, I continued,

"Baba! Khidr brought me the calm waters of love. In his company, I found peace that I had never felt before. But now in his absence, I am drowning in the deep waters of sorrow."

---

[3] Dunya is an Arabic word for 'material world'

"My dear Child! Let sorrow be your companion and not your enemy. Accept it and do not resist it in the journey of love. This pain shuffles the life around you, makes you question, makes you wonder, makes you ponder. It shakes the unessential dust which scuttles the innocence of your heart and makes room for the beauty of love to reside." Baba said.

I nodded silently and continued. "Before I met Khidr, I was doing everything that I had always wanted to. I was living the life of my choice, in the way that I had wanted to. Nothing was lacking in my life, yet a deep void within my heart haunted me. It was Khidr who filled that void. He was the one who, in the short period that I spent with him, made me feel complete. I felt like a long yearning of my soul had finally come to rest. I had never felt so seen and safe in my life. But now his sudden absence has wrecked my heart, broken my spirit and pierced my soul. So despaired and uprooted I feel Baba, that now I wish I had never met him!" My desperation and gloom had made me say the unspeakable. I was surprised and ashamed at my own words, but Baba listened to them with the same placidity. He continued,

"Dear Child, we do not get to choose the people who come or leave our lives. But what we do get to choose is whether we remember or forget them, and if we do remember, what and how we remember them. However, each person whom we meet in this life has a role to play and has something to teach. Be grateful to him."

"But Baba! I am not just pained by the separation from my beloved but also hurt by his harshness. I know the love we share is too deep to be doubted, but why did Khidr abandon me all alone?"

"My Child! I am sure your beloved has not abandoned you, for if he had, you wouldn't be thinking of him so fondly, would you? Truth is, your heart knows that he is still with you; only you cannot see him yet in person. Always remember, love is not a claim but a gift; it comes not by command but by surrender."

Reassuring me, Baba further said, "I know your mind is trapped in a web of doubts. But maybe this is exactly what you need to overcome in this journey. Always remember, if love is true, it will be tested. If you ever feel alone in this test, always trust that you will be accompanied by your beloved, if not today, then tomorrow. But trust you must."

"I believe you, Baba, but he left without saying a word? Did I not deserve at least a goodbye from him?"

"Maybe, he was sure of returning very soon? Maybe he felt a goodbye would only hurt you more? The possibilities are endless; it is up to you what you want to believe." Baba then looked at me deeply and, closing his eyes, asked me, "When we love someone deeply with our heart and soul, do we ever separate from them? Then, where does the need for goodbye arise anyway?"

"If there is no separation, why haven't I met my beloved yet?" I sobbed.

"Open your eyes, listen to your heart, and when you accept the flow of life, you will realise that you do not have to meet him, he is already with you. Ask yourself if your bond with Khidr depends on his mere physical presence or the love between both of you? And if your answer is the latter, you will know that the bond has very little to do with his physical presence. True lovers always exist within each other; they do not have to meet, for they are never separate from each other", Baba said.

"Lovers don't finally meet somewhere. They're in each other all along." Maulana's words resounded in my ears. "So, Baba, you are asking me to return home without finding my love?"

"How can you find your lover when you have never lost him in the first place? You do not have to seek your lover, but to realise what causes this distance between you and your beloved. It is the mind, the knowledge, the fear which causes this restlessness, but your heart always knows. It is time for you to reject this restlessness. It is time for you to return home, dear Child!"

"I cannot think clearly. My mind is obscured, my vision is blurred, and my soul is tormented. But I will listen to your counsel, Baba. I trust your wisdom." I bowed before Baba.

"Before you leave, tell me one thing, Child, when you want to see your appearance, what do you search for?" Baba asked in his same calm tone.

"I search for a mirror."

"Exactly, when you cannot see yourself clearly, seek a mirror, not merely to see the appearance of your face but of your heart."

"And where does one find mirrors of the heart?"

"Well, in the hearts of other men. We get to know ourselves from the mirrors in the hearts of other men"

I nodded softly and prepared to leave when Baba suddenly handed me a small bag filled with eatables and bread. He smiled at me with affection, and my eyes welled up, touched by his care.

I bid him goodbye. When I looked back after taking a few steps, I saw him waving still with thoughtful eyes. A gentle smile played on his lips.

On walking further ahead, I looked back again, but the path was engulfed in white mist. I tried hard to trace him, but Baba was not visible any more.

A long and lonely path ahead stared back at me, and I knew I had to walk it all alone by myself. "It's your road, and yours alone. Others may walk it with you, but no one can walk it for you." Maulana's words came to me again, and I continued to walk ahead.

Way Back Home

My way back towards home surprisingly did not feel as awkward as I was expecting. I was returning after a very long, arduous journey. I had spent months walking alone in search of Khidr. There were days I walked incessantly without food and water. My body was stretched to its limits of endurance. There were times when I doubted if I would survive. I suffered this tough ordeal only because I wanted to find Khidr. But there I was, returning home, having 'failed' to achieve the very aim I had embarked on this journey for. Strangely, though, the 'failure' did not feel as debilitating as one would have expected it to. In fact, I felt unusually and inexplicably content as I walked back towards my home.

My interaction with Baba had deeply changed my perspective and instilled an unshakeable faith in my destiny. A profound sense of acceptance pervaded my being, and I was ready to receive with gratitude whatever destiny had in store for me.

“We have to wander somewhere very far to reach somewhere very close.” Baba’s words echoed in my ears as I paced my walk towards home.

The Stream

Logically, the way back to my home should have felt easier to trace but I unexpectedly felt lost. I didn't know which way or route to take.

I kept walking dazed and confused, when suddenly my eyes lit up seeing a beautiful stream running at a distance. I was fairly confident it was the same stream which ran close to my home and which I had often seen during the previous course of my journey. I was elated to see the stream and started walking along with it, with firm belief that it would lead me to the right path.

Journey Towards Home

While my journey back to home started with slow heavy steps, I quickly picked up pace on the way. Baba's profound words and benevolent visage lingered in my heart and encouraged me to move ahead with renewed enthusiasm. However, as time lapsed, my body's energy reserves began to deplete. I started to feel hungry and suddenly remembered the food that Baba had handed over to me.

I decided to sit close to the stream to have food. I bowed over the waters to wash my face and was surprised to see my reflection. The long days of physical strain, fatigue and stress had taken a toll on my health, and I visibly looked frail and feeble. I touched my pale face with despair. "Seek a mirror to see not just the appearance of your face but of your heart”, I remembered Baba’s advice.

“Hello there, beautiful miss!” Suddenly, an animated male voice came from far right behind the woods. “What brings you to these lonesome jungles?” the voice continued.

Startled, I looked up in fear.

A Chance Encounter

A man, aged about thirty, appeared from behind the trees flashing a wide grin on his face.

Reading my fear and discomfort, he quickly added "Oh please don't be worried, Miss. I mean no harm. Please don't misunderstand. I was just pleasantly surprised to see a human company in these desolate jungles. You see, I am a modest carpenter, but *(winking)* ironically, I do not like to cut trees. I venture deep into the jungles to find fallen logs and collect them to be carried to my shop in the town.

There are thicker trees close to the stream, so I usually come this way. I fix one day in a month for collecting the logs, and then the next day I come with my fellows to take them to town. It is a laborious process, you see, but what to do? I have to do it!" He said, stretching his already wide grin. "Usually, it gets very monotonous to search logs in these mysterious, desolate jungles, so I was thrilled to see another, err… very beautiful human being here, and I just exclaimed in excitement! I am a little impulsive that way! He he he!" he laughed nervously, "I never intended to surprise you and sorry if I did, in the wrong way! He he he.." he continued chattering, in an embarrassed tone.

My stomach was growling with hunger, and the talkative carpenter was showing no sign of pausing, so I interrupted him midway, "Sorry, but I am very hungry. I need to eat now. It was, eh.., nice to meet you," I mustered a smile.

"Oh yes! Oh yes! You must, you must. Well, would you mind if I join you for lunch as well?"

I unknowingly gave him a questioning look

"Oh, don't worry, I have brought my lunch." He grinned again, but seeing my doubtful expression, he amusingly altered his talking style in a flash and whispered in a serious tone, "Trust me, food tastes much better when had in company"

His jolly tantrums and antics broke me into a hearty laughter, and I realised it was probably the first time since the beginning of my journey that I had laughed so deeply.

I at once felt very grateful to this stranger carpenter for making me laugh after so long. I noticed he was happy to see me laughing, too.

"What is your name?" I asked

"Well, Miss, this humble bloke is called Kareem," he answered, flashing the same wide grin and bowing a *salaam*.

"Nice name, Kareem, 'the kind one'… well, I am…." I was about to introduce myself when he interrupted.

"Oh, wait, wait, let me take a guess at your name. A beautiful girl, so gentle and kind, delicate like a fairy, so thoughtful in her ways, with deep soulful eyes, laughter like a gush of river, gaze as deep as oceans. What could the world call you? Umm.. Roohi?"

My jaw dropped in consternation.

Mixed feelings of surprise, joy, embarrassment and fear, overcame me.

"How do you know my name? Who…who are you?" I stammered, trying to compose myself.

"Why, is that actually your name?" Kareem chuckled and looked astonished himself. Too stunned by the unbelievable coincidence, I was unable to reciprocate his laughter and stood stiff.

"Come on, this was just a coincidence! I just thought the name perfectly described your persona, and lo and behold, it turned out to be your actual name!" Kareem casually waved his hand in the air, a wide, generous smile still playing on his lips.

Too hungry to ponder more over this happenstance, we both sat down to eat.

The Meal

The beautiful stream was flowing quietly besides us. It was afternoon time and the sun was shining brightly. The winds flowed pleasantly under the shades of thick woods, and birds chirped mellow tones of afternoon calm.

I opened the food wrapped in soft velvet cloth. The bread smelled fresh and warm, although I was opening it after hours. The fritters were crisp and golden, and citrus fruits shone in vibrant colours. Tangy spicy pickles were wrapped carefully in one of the breads. I spread out the appetising meal and invited Kareem to share food with me. He had also opened his meals, which looked equally delicious.

Master and Disciple

The food Baba gave me was divinely delicious, specially the bread. It had aroma of unique herbs that I had never tasted before. With each morsel my spirit and body felt more refreshed and energised.

While eating, I noticed Kareem's face closely. Short trimmed hair, sleek moustache, dark brown tanned complexion, clean shaven. He looked fairly handsome. He was a man of average build and medium height. An enthusiastic smile almost always played on his lips. His deep, dark eyes, however, betrayed his easy-going and relaxed nature and hinted at an intense and deeply thinking mind behind his cheerful persona.

"Hey, please eat, what are you thinking? Aren't you hungry?" Kareem asked as he took one piece of bread from mine. As he tasted my bread, his expression suddenly turned nostalgic, as if the taste reminded him of something special.

I, too, picked up a piece of bread from his meal, and I was surprised that it tasted exactly like the bread prepared by Baba. Our gazes met each other for a moment as if exchanging an unspoken epiphany.

"Who cooked your bread?" I asked, surprised.

"Well! I have prepared it. I cook for myself. And your bread.... let me guess... Baba made it for you?"

"How do you know Baba?" I asked, flabbergasted once again at the recurring coincidences.

Kareem replied with a carefree wave, "Well, didn't I tell you, I have been visiting these jungles for many years?" Turning contemplative, he continued, "I met him during one of my visits here, at a time which was probably the lowest point of my life. I earnestly needed counsel, a guide to walk me past the quagmire of thoughts I had landed myself in. And unexpectedly, he found me. I have learnt many things in life from Baba, including baking this bread."

"I too found Baba, or rather Baba found me too in a similar manner, when I needed him the most" I reflected.

Taste and Temptation

Happy and amused at the series of coincidences, we ate our lunch together in the quiet peace of the woods. While eating we shared our life stories, laughed at silly jokes and reminisced about old memories. The soft gush of the stream added a charming music to the scenic landscape. Kareem's gentle and kind nature made my heart feel light and easy. His carefree ways and cheerful demeanour soothed all my worries and brought me a calm which I had missed for so long.

Kareem caught me looking at him intently and reciprocated with a reflective smile. As we finished eating and started packing up our belongings quietly, the sky suddenly turned dark and it began to rain unexpectedly.

Surprised by the sudden change of weather, we rushed under a nearby tree. Kareem stood protectively near me, trying to shield me from the voracious winds. He was no longer the same carefree man I saw a short while ago, but looked concerned and serious, trying to take care of me. The winds blew wildly for the next several minutes. We stood still against the trunk of the tree, braving the force of the storm. The winds were so strong that I was afraid to be blown away, but Kareem held me strongly.

After a reckless spell, the rains subsided, and he heaved a sigh. Holding me still, he asked, "Are you okay?"

I nodded quietly.

"Rains were not expected today, much less a storm…The logs must have got wet…" he remembered.

"Oh, I am sorry that your visit went in vain today", I whispered.

Looking deep into my eyes, he softly replied, "Oh no, not at all. On the contrary, this was a special visit, as it led me to meet you."

Our eyes remained transfixed at each other, and we came closer. Kareem was still holding me by my waist, and I was leaning onto his shoulders. His face was washed with raindrops, and his hair was swept back. I could feel his warm breath on my face. We leaned closer, our lips almost touching. I felt a wave of passion surging in me and a temptation to give in. Just then, lightning struck in the sky, and I was saved from drowning in the wave.

I pulled myself out of Kareem's embrace. My eyes lowered, I said, "I thank you so much, Kareem, for your friendship. I thank you for reminding me of my laughter and the beauty of my heart, which I had forgotten. You touched me with your care and affection. But now it is time for me to return home."

We stood quietly in silence. Our hearts needed that space to accept our inevitable reality. The time for us to part ways had arrived. It was hard to believe that we had met only for a few hours, and yet this bond felt ages old.

"Would you like to walk the path ahead with me, Roohi?" He asked, his voice quivering with the pain of our imminent separation.

"No, Kareem, some journeys are for us to complete alone. Khidr is not with me, but my heart belongs to him. My journey is not complete unless I find him, and no one can do it for me, except me and me alone."

We were both crying now. After a pause, Kareem continued, "I accept your decision, Roohi and I wish you nothing but the best in your journey ahead. This heart will cry for you, but I can explain it to calm down. This mind will remember you, but I will convince it to forget you, but you, my dear, have touched my soul. And there is no way to explain to the soul. Soul cannot be convinced. And so, I will continue to love you in silence, for as Maulana says, in silence there is no rejection."

We looked at each other one last time. With tears rolling down our cheeks, we bid each other goodbye.

My meeting with Kareem, his kindness and affection, my fondness for his company, his proposal, its rejection and our parting; these series of events made me realise how deeply I loved Khidr. Despite the heartbreak and the pain, I felt a stronger conviction in my resolve to find Khidr.

In life, one has to learn to balance 'holding on' and 'letting go'; Maulana's verses again came to my rescue. I remembered them and continued my journey ahead.

Walk Towards Home

I continued walking along the stream with mixed emotions. On one hand my journey was coming to an end, on the other, I knew it was not the end until I found Khidr.

Despite the setbacks, the biggest being the fact that Khidr was not with me yet, this journey had given me many gifts. It tested the limits of my patience, it brought me closer to Maulana, I walked in sync with nature, met a soul-guide in the form of Baba, heard his stirring discourse and formed a memorable friendship with Kareem. I had a lot to be grateful for.

A sense of calm relief and contentment swept over me, and I paced my steps towards home.

Reaching Home

After days of walking, I was finally close to my home. With the stream as my guide, I could map in my mind the route to reach home. I took a final turn away from the stream to head closer towards home.

After walking a little more, I was able to see my house at some distance, atop the hill. From the blurry vision of my welled-up eyes, I could see the surrounding fences, the trees, the roof and the kitchen.

I could see Simfi, standing near the fence, wagging her tail frantically, as if she had been waiting for my return for a long. As soon as I came closer, she ran towards me excitedly. With tears running down our faces, we both embraced each other tightly, longer than ever before.

Overwhelmed by an array of emotions and with Simfi frolicking beside me, I took dizzy steps ahead and the next moment I found myself standing in front of the door to my house. After pausing for a second, I pushed the door to open it. But to my surprise, it did not open.

Dismayed, I looked at Simfi with confusion, but she meekly let out an ignorant moan.

A Knock Again

I pushed the door again but it still did not open. Someone had obviously latched it from inside.

I knocked the door agitatedly and asked, "Who is it?"

"It is you", answered a soft, gentle male voice from inside. I was awestruck, my breath paused, and my heart skipped a beat. The voice was not of a stranger but the one that I had been yearning to hear for the longest time.

The door flung open the next moment, and Khidr was standing in front of me. His lips were curved into a smile, but his eyes conveyed an intensity that no words could articulate. His face furrowed with pain, regret and longing, he rushed towards me and I embraced him tightly. Overwhelmed, we cried together, not uttering a word. Simfi stood silently beside us, her tail drooped down.

When the flow of tears paused, Khidr took me inside the house.

I was still processing the sudden turn of events, and it felt as if I was living a dream. My joy knew no bounds after meeting Khidr.

The Union

Everything was just the same inside as it was when I left the house. Khidr held my hand and made me sit comfortably in the armchair that stood opposite the window. The sun was about to set, and the sky had turned tangerine. Soft golden rays of the sun were falling on me, and I felt cosy, soaking in the warmth of the sun. Khidr brought me a tumbler of water and settled on the stool, facing me. He was wearing the same off-white robe tied in the waist by a string, his hair shining in the sunlight; he looked as divinely handsome as the day when we first met, or even more.

He looked at me affectionately. I could ask Khidr a million questions, but at that moment I felt as if all my words had dried up. In meeting him, all the questions now felt obsolete. We sat quietly in the golden sunlight while Simfi lay smugly outside, as if allowing us our moments of privacy. Khidr finally broke the silence,

"I am sorry for the pain I have caused you, Roohi. There is no word and no repentance enough to compensate for this sin.

But if it may make you feel any better, let me share that in each moment of your absence, I have lived only for you. After I left that day, I struggled to sleep through a single night and struggled to survive through each day. It is only the hope to see you again that has not let me slip away.

Every moment of that night is clear in my mind. I remember the moment when you slept in my arms and I kissed your forehead. Your tender skin shone in the moonlight, and your lips quivered like fresh petals. Your long golden - brown tresses had wrapped my arms, and your lustrous form dazzled beside me. You looked so beautiful, like an angel to me.

I gazed at you, spellbound by your ethereal beauty. As much as I admired your fairy-like charm, it suddenly began to evoke in me a sense of unworthiness. I began to question myself if I really deserved your company, your beauty, your touch, much less your love. You slept next to me like an angel in human form, and there I was, a man unsure of his own self. I did not deserve an angel like you, or rather, you did not deserve a directionless man like me! A strong sense of self-loathing took over me, and I felt I could not face you anymore. I stood up abruptly and ran away without looking back."

He paused and looked at me, probably anticipating a reaction, but too overwhelmed to respond, I could only manage a faint nod.

He continued:

"I ran towards the jungle and kept running for a long time until I realised Simfi was following me. When I looked back at her, she wagged her tail, as if asking me to go no further. I stopped and spent the night in the jungle in Simfi's comforting company.

Although I did not feel courageous enough to face you, yet I did not want to go very far away from you. I was trapped in a strange paradox. I felt deep love for you in my heart, yet I did not feel worthy myself to receive the same from you.

And for the next many days, every night I would return to the same spot in the jungle, where Simfi would be waiting for me. I would visit this house late past midnight and look at you from outside through the window. I saw you thus each night, on your bed deep in sleep, just the way you had slept in my arms that day."

He looked at me again, my eyes were wide in dismay, yet I could not say a word. A drop of tear rolled down my face.

"You visited me every night?" I questioned in disbelief.

Nodding and teary-eyed, Khidr continued:

"Yes! Each night, while coming towards the house, I would make up my mind to wake you from your sleep and seek your forgiveness. But the moment I would look at your beautiful face deep in sleep, I would lose my courage, fearing my actions might hurt you more than my absence. And thus, I would return to the jungles each night silently after just looking at you from outside the window. Every such silent return from this house dimmed my confidence further, and I plummeted into the dark depths of despair. I moved towards the town, picked up odd jobs and earned some money. But each night I would return to the jungles, meet Simfi and complete my daily ritual to get your glimpse while you were fast asleep."

My eyes were fixed on Khidr, still processing his words. It was difficult for me to come to terms with the fact that every single day that I missed him terribly, he had been so close to me, without me ever realising it.

Khidr was seemingly burning with guilt and avoided my disbelieving gaze.

"And Simfi? She knew about you and did not give me a hint? I feel so betrayed by both of you," I asked, barely withholding my resentment.

"I understand you are upset, Roohi, and your anger is very well justified. But please hear me out fully, and then I will be willing to accept whatever you decide." After a brief pause, Khidr continued, "Yes, Simfi knew about me, but maybe she knew much more than both of us. She probably knew that it was not the right time yet for us to meet and waited for the right moment to arrive."

I looked at Simfi's big, deep eyes and couldn't help but agree with Khidr. She was much wiser than I had anticipated. I kept silent. Khidr continued to speak with lowered gaze, and I listened to him with bated breath.

"This ritual of my visits continued for many days until one day Simfi came looking for me in the town while I was busy with some work. One look at her and I instantly knew something was not right, for she never came to meet me in the daytime. She was panting restlessly, and her eyes looked lost. I ran to the house with her and saw the doors latched from the outside. I instantly knew you had left, and I also understood why."

Khidra's voice shook as he ended his statement, and he sobbed softly.

"Aghast at your leaving, I collapsed on the ground and fainted. When I regained consciousness, Simfi was sitting next to me. I had lost all the will to live. Filled with great shame and grief, I got up to leave this place, but it was Simfi who stopped me. Surprisingly, she pulled the end of my robe with her teeth and refused to let me go. She stretched my robe in the direction of this house and led me to the door. I looked at her; her eyes were fixed on me, and her tail was wagging frantically as if waiting for me to open the door.

I hesitantly opened the door. Simfi continued to look at me intensely and woofed louder, as if directing me to step inside. As soon as I stepped in, she jumped in too, her tail wagging swiftly still, as if encouraging me to stay.

I looked around. The house was resounding with your absence, yet your presence could be felt so strongly inside the house. Your table, your books, your chair, your pen, this stool, every iota of this house was immersed in your presence. As I looked at each object of the house around, feeling your warm presence, I felt myself becoming a part of this house too. Your presence filled my very being. My life changed completely in that moment of epiphany.

In that magical moment, I felt you so deeply in and around me that there arose no question of going anywhere. Since that day I have been here, waiting for you while carrying you in every pore of my being.

Ever since I came, I kept everything just the way it was when you left. Feeling your presence so deeply here gave me hope that I shall meet you again. My will to live returned. I wanted to live to wait for you, to meet you, to find you again. I found myself thus in finding you. Dissolved in your presence thus, I became you."

Khidr's narration of his experience led me to a sudden realisation, and I interrupted him suddenly.

"Oh! Is that why you replied "you" when I knocked on the door and asked 'Who's it?"

Nodding in affirmation, Khidr replied unassumingly, "Yes, because when you asked, I could only find you within me. 'I' had dissolved long back."

Flooded with emotions, I wanted to say countless words but could form none. Sensing this, Khidr diverted my attention, pointing outside the window

"Look over there. As I started staying here, I took to farming. I have grown rice, legumes and some vegetables too. See, how lush has been the yield"

I saw the verdant farms outside the window, swaying with the winds, glowing in the fading light of sunset.

"It was like an awakening. I had never done farming before in my life. But as I returned to this house, I felt like my life had discovered its purpose. I found the direction that I was looking for. Farming brought me peace and purpose to my existence. I no longer felt like a directionless man, as I did before. I felt I was finally worthy to wait for you and found the courage to face you.

The pain of longing became my cure, and I longed for you, knowing that you would come one day. And that day is today."

He looked at me and stood up.

All my doubts, anger and resentment melted away in the warmth of his brave honesty. The entire cosmos seemed to reverberate in celebratory ecstasy.

I rushed towards Khidr and embraced him warmly. The sky outside turned dark violet, and stars twinkled brightly. Simfi looked on, her ears taut and eyes delighted.

The flame in the fire pit crackled softly, and the full moon shone from the window as we kissed each other, rediscovering the epicentre of our shared existence.

"At the end of my life, with just one breath left,
if you come, I'll sit up and sing."
-Rumi